Trixie and the Tiger

by Victoria Cabassa
pictures by Lilian Obligado

Abelard-Schuman
London New York Toronto

©Copyright 1967, text by Victoria Cabassa
©Copyright 1967, illustrations by Lilian Obligado
Library of Congress Catalogue Card Number: 67-19609
First published in Great Britain in 1968
Standard Book No. 200.71511.9
Printed in the United States of America

8679

A Tiger lived under Trixie's bed.
It was quiet there, and warm,
with soft dark shadows
like a little jungle.

Trixie begged the Tiger to come out.
"Please come walking with me.
I won't let anyone hurt you.
I like you, Tiger."

But the Tiger would
not come out.

The Tiger slapped his long thick tail
on the floor. He stuck the tip of his
black nose out . . . just a little.

He growled way down
low in his throat.
"Grr-grr-rr," he said.
That meant, "No!"

Trixie went to school.
She told her friends,
"I have a Tiger. He lives under my bed.
He is a very nice Tiger."

Nobody believed her.
"Tigers live in cages.
You can see them at the Zoo.
But under beds . . . NEVER.
We don't believe you,"
the children sang, over and over
and over and over and over again.

The Teacher clapped her hands.
"Now stop! All of you!
Trixie," she said, "you don't really
have a Tiger under your bed."

"But I *do!*" whispered Trixie to herself.

At bedtime that night, Trixie
bounced into bed with a big thump.
The Tiger growled and growled, but he
did not come out from under the bed.
"You were very troublesome today, Tiger,"
said Trixie. "Very, very troublesome."

"Grrrrr," said the Tiger.

The next day, the Teacher read a story to
the class. It was all about a wicked tiger
who lived far away in a hot dense jungle.
This tiger was a bad beast. He chased
people. The people ran away fast because
they were afraid.

The little boys and girls listened to
the story. Their eyes were big with wonder.
"What a terrible, *terrible* animal
the tiger is," they said.

But Trixie shook her head and said,
"My Tiger is not a bit wicked.
My Tiger would not chase people.
My Tiger is afraid of people.
That is why he stays under my bed."

"Gosh, what a fib," said the children.
The Teacher closed her book and looked
at the class.
"Now stop, all of you," she said.

Later that day the Teacher made an
announcement.
"Tomorrow each of you may bring a pet to school.
Then you may tell one story about your pet.
I will judge both the pet and the story."
Everyone talked at once.
"I have the best puppy in the whole
world," said a little boy.
"Oh, no!" said a little girl, "I have the best."

When Trixie went home, she looked under her bed.
"Tiger," she called softly. "Oh, Tiger."
There was no answer.
"Please growl, Tiger," she begged.
But the Tiger did not growl.
Trixie waited a little while and then she
looked again.

There was no Tiger under the bed.
There was a sock with holes. There was
an old shoe without a lace.
But there was no Tiger.

The next morning, it was very noisy at school.
The children made noise—so did all the pets.
"QUIET!" said the Teacher. "QUIET, I say."

A boy brought a big dog over to the Teacher's desk.
He told a story about the way it buries its bones.
A girl brought a chipmunk in a cage to the Teacher's
desk. She told a story about the way the
chipmunk begs for sunflower seeds.

Everyone brought a pet except Trixie.

"Don't you have a pet, Trixie?" the Teacher asked.

"I have my Tiger," said Trixie. "The one I told you about. The one who lives under my bed."

"Yah," yelled the boys. "Why didn't you bring your Tiger?"

The girls just giggled.

Trixie looked around the room.
There were no striped paws. There was no
striped tail. There was no soft growl.
There were no orangy and black stripes.

There was no Tiger there at all.
"Never mind," said the Teacher.

"Oh, my Tiger wanted to come," said Trixie.
"But he couldn't."
"Tell me later, Trixie," said the Teacher.
"My Tiger had a toothache," Trixie went on.
"He cried all night. I took him to the Zoo."
The Teacher stood up and clapped her hands.
"It is time to go home, children. Let's tidy up."

"But I *would* have taken my Tiger to the Zoo
if he had a toothache," Trixie said to herself
on the way home.

The following morning, the Teacher said, "I have another surprise for you. We have been given tickets to visit the Zoo. We will have our lunch there, and we will see all the animals."
Everyone was delighted.

The children marched out, two by two. The
Teacher walked ahead.
"Follow me," she said, and stepped smartly
along the street.
She turned around now and then to count noses.
There were twenty-two boys and girls.

Soon they entered the park. Flowers grew
everywhere.
The Teacher stopped and counted again.
This time she counted twenty-one noses . . .
and a bouquet.
"Trixie," she said sternly, "what are you
up to now?"
"I am picking flowers for my Tiger," said
Trixie.
The children giggled.
The Teacher just looked up at the sky,
and said, "My goodness gracious me."

From a stone building nearby, a lion roared.
"Let's see the lions," cried some of the children.
"And the tigers," cried the rest of the children.
But Trixie made a big flower fan and covered
her face.

There was one tiger.
He was big.
He had big paws.
A big tail.
Big eyes.
Big teeth.
A big head.
Big ears.
A big bunch of orangy and black stripes.

"Is this *your* Tiger, Trixie?" asked the children.
Trixie peeped through the flowers.
"No," she said. "My Tiger came home last night.
This tiger is *not* my Tiger."

Later, on the way home, Trixie looked
in the window of a pet shop.
She saw puppies. They barked and wagged
their little tails.
She saw a myna bird.
He talked to her.
But she did not see her Tiger.

"Was your Tiger home?" asked one of the girls
the next day.

"Yes," said Trixie. "He was playing in our yard."

"Trixie," said the Teacher, "was he really?"

"Oh, all right," said Trixie. "My Tiger was
not playing in our yard."

"But he will be," she thought to herself.

On Saturday the doorbell rang.
It was the Teacher.
Trixie asked her to come in and sit down on
the big red sofa.
Trixie called her mother and then she went up
to her room. She washed her hands and brushed
her teeth and put on a clean dress. She combed
her hair a little bit.
Then she went back downstairs.

"Trixie," said the Teacher, "would you like
to go to the circus with me?"
Trixie nodded yes.
She and the Teacher walked three blocks and
then took a bus.
On the way, they saw a few dogs and a bushy-tailed
squirrel.
"We will see tigers at the circus, Trixie," said
the Teacher. "Perhaps we will see your
Tiger there, too."

Trixie and the Teacher sat in the front
row. They ate popcorn and candy and peanuts
and hot dogs. They drank fruit juice from
little paper cups.
They saw bareback riders, and dogs that
did tricks, and elephants that danced, and
clowns who fell down, and pretty girls in
pink tights, and handsome men in green tights,
and horses prancing around and around.
It was very pleasant.

Suddenly, there were tigers.
Three of them.
They were safe in a huge cage with
iron bars.
The cage with the tigers in it was
rolled up close to the front row and
a man with a chair was inside.
The man spoke to the tigers and they
jumped up on stools and looked right
at Trixie.

"Is your Tiger here?" asked the Teacher.
Trixie looked at each tiger.
The first tiger was big and ferocious.

The second tiger was big and ferocious.
So was the third tiger.
Trixie shook her head.
"No, my Tiger is not here," she told the
Teacher.
"I think I know where your Tiger might be,"
said the Teacher. "Come with me."
The Teacher hailed a taxi and got in with Trixie.
They drove through the streets and stopped
at a white house with a spacious green lawn.
They got out and walked down a shady lane
until they came to a barn.

It was dark in the barn—a soft warm dark.
A furry tiger was stretched out on some hay.
Little tigers played about.
"Meow-w-w," said the little tigers.
The big tiger growled pleasantly and slapped
her tail at the hay.
The Teacher picked up a little tiger and
placed it in Trixie's arms. "Is this
your Tiger?" she asked.

Trixie carried him to the light and looked
him over very carefully.
He had a long tail and soft ears and orangy
and black stripes. He purred gently.
"Oh, yes!" she said. "This IS MY
VERY OWN TIGER."

That night, Trixie went to bed happy.
There were soft muffled sounds under her bed,
as if a Tiger were hunting for his food.
Then, there was a sound of snoring, as if a
tired Tiger had fallen asleep.
It was a nice sound.
To Trixie, it was the nicest
sound in all the world.